Kingd...
A Lesso... y

Writt...

D1307213

ISBN: 154538584X
ISBN-13: 978-1545385845

DEDICATION

This book is dedicated to all of the Kingdom Warriors in this world. We all have a part to play and however small it seems to be we are working towards the same ultimate goal.

1 Corinthians 12:4-11

Glory to God, who is able to do far beyond all that we could ask or imagine by his power at work within us.

Ephesians 3:20

ACKNOWLEDGMENTS

I would first like to thank my husband, Joe, without whom any of this would be possible. I am truly blessed to have you in my life. Thank you, Coco, for all of your help. Thank you to my friends, who offered encouragement on this venture. I would also like to thank my instructor, Keith Yates, for starting me on the path that led to where I am now. If you had not invested in my martial arts training, none of this would have come to fruition.

I am incredibly grateful for all of you.

It was a busy Friday afternoon at DMD Martial Arts, and all of the students were excited for the big tournament the following day. They had been working so hard this past month, and though they felt prepared, they were still very nervous.

"What do you think it's going to be like?" Cathy whispered to her sister, Rosemary, as they practiced self-defense.

"I don't know Cathy, but I'm sure glad I'll be watching you compete." she replied with a grin.

A couple rows down, Ryan and Riley were discussing the same. "I can't wait to compete in sparring!" Ryan said. "What about you? Did you decide if you're going to compete?"
"I don't think so," replied Riley. "It's not really my thing."
"Too bad," Ryan said with a slight shake of his head. "You're missing out."

"Yame!" Sensei called over the chatter. "Bow to your partners, and line up. Seiretsu."

All the students bowed to each other then ran into one line, in order from highest to lowest rank.

"Students, I am so proud of all of your efforts in preparation for this tournament tomorrow. You have all worked so hard. I know tournaments are exciting, but they are also scary, aren't they?"

"Hai, Sensei!" the students replied in near-unison.

"I know you have many things on your mind," the instructor continued. "You are worried how your kata looks, you are worried about scoring the most points in sparring, right? And I am sure you are all hoping to bring home a trophy. But students, that is not the most important thing, and what I want you all to learn from this experience is that we are not going to this tournament to bring glory to ourselves, but to our Father above."

David raised his hand.

"Yes, David." Sensei said.

"Does that mean we're bringing glory to God by kicking and punching the other kids?" He had a puzzled look on his face.

"No, sir," the instructor answered with a chuckle. "It most certainly does not! What I meant was that we would present ourselves in a manner to which He would be pleased. We will be on our best behavior, and will be clothed in humility."

"But sir," David continued. "I don't want to be embarrassed!"

"You don't need to be, David. You see, humility is not the same thing as embarrassment. Can anyone tell me the opposite of humility?"

Eliana raised her hand straight away.
"Yes, Eliana."
"Pride." she said, nodding her head in finality.
"You are absolutely right. Students, did you know pride was the very first sin?"
The students looked to each other in wonder.

"Many of you are probably thinking it was eating the forbidden apple, aren't you? Disobeying? But in truth, pride was the very first. And God warns us about pride in many, many verses. For example, Philippians 2:3 says 'Don't do anything for selfish purposes, but with humility think of others as better than yourselves.' In Proverbs 16:18, the Bible says, 'Pride comes before disaster, and arrogance before a fall,' the instructor added.

Therefore, if there is any encouragement in Christ, any comfort in love, any sharing in the Spirit, any sympathy, complete my joy by thinking the same way, having the same love, being united, and agreeing with each other.

Philippians 2:3
Don't do anything for selfish purposes, but with humility think of others as better than yourselves.

Instead of each person watching out for their own good, watch out for what is better for others.

"But sir!" Elizabeth said as she raised her hand. "Does that mean that if we work really hard, like we did for the tournament, that we can't be proud of what we accomplish?"

"No, Elizabeth, but that is a very good question. You see, pride comes from our ego, and it comes when we choose not to acknowledge where our gifts truly come from. In fact, I have a very good story about humility, and if you all have a couple extra minutes, I'd love to share it with you."

Sensei looked to the lobby, and the parents waiting up front nodded in affirmation.

Sensei looked to David as he began, "Do you remember the story of Daniel in Babylon? How he was taken to serve King Nebuchadnezzar?"

David nodded with a smile, as well as a couple other students, but some looked a little puzzled.

He continued, "Well, Daniel had been in Babylon several years by now, and despite the past events, he and the King were fairly close. You see, the King trusted Daniel's gift of understanding dreams, and he knew that David gave him sound advice over the years, not to his own benefit. One night, the King had another dream about a tree that grew in size and power. But a Being came down from Heaven and said the tree must be cut down, but that its roots were to be left alone. Furthermore, the stump was to be bound in iron and bronze."

The students listened, mesmerized.

"Then, the heavenly Being spoke about the tree as if it were a man. He said that its mind must be changed to that of an animal for seven years. Now that's something, isn't it students?"

They all nodded in agreement but kept their eyes on him. They wanted to know the end of the story!

"Daniel trusted in God for his gift of interpreting dreams, and this was no exception. He was able to surmise that the dream was pointing to the pride of King Nebuchadnezzar. You see, the dream was a warning for him to change his ways, or that he would be punished. The King was, unfortunately, a very prideful man. He was very accomplished, yes, but he refused to share the glory with the One who truly gave it to him.

Often, the King would conduct tours of his kingdom, bragging about his newly restored temples, his great bridge over the Euphrates River, his Ishtar Gate, and the extravagant gardens he had built for his wife.

His arrogance and pride were his downfall."

Ryan raised his hand. "Sir, what happened in the end?"

"Just as the prophesy told, Ryan. He was turned into a wild beast for 7 years."

The students looked wide-eyed at the instructor as he wrapped up. "Students, the most important thing you can do at the tournament tomorrow is to bring your humility with you. It is all I ask, and all I want to see. Being the best in kata and sparring is nothing compared to giving the glory where it is truly due. And we do that by remembering where our talents truly come from. Understood?"

"Hai, Sensei!" the students called.

Riley raised his hand slowly. "Sir, where in the Bible was that story?"

"Daniel 4:1-37, Riley."

"Thank you, sir."

The instructor nodded and smiled. Everyone bowed out. Then came the expected rush of students grabbing their things and heading out the door.

Saturday came. Despite the instructor's message the day before, the students were still nervous as they entered the arena where the tournament was held. Everywhere they looked, they saw students from other schools, showcasing their best.

Kim, Elizabeth, Jen, Eliana, David, Cathy, and Ryan all made it through registration. They were intimidated with all the noise and activity going on. In one corner, brown belts were competing in kata. Their precision and skills were inspiring! On the other side of the room, sparring competitions were going on. Though the competitors were only intermediate belts, the students of DMD Martial Arts saw that contact was allowed!

Despite their anxiousness, the students tried to remember Sensei's words the day before.

"Exciting, isn't it?" the instructor said, as he walked up behind the group.   Just hearing his voice amidst all the noise around them made the students breathe a sigh of relief.

The students split off into their assigned rings, and waited for their turns to compete in kata.

Eliana sat down next to a boy one belt higher than she. She turned towards him to wish him well.

"Good luck on your kata!" She almost had to yell to make her voice rise above the noise around them.

The boy next to her looked at her as if she were a nuisance.

"What kata are *you* doing?" he asked in a not-so-polite tone.

"I'm doing Heian Yodan," she replied. "What about you? Are you doing Heian Godan?"

"No, *I'm* doing Tekki Sandan." he remarked in a superior tone. "My instructor taught me some more advanced katas so I could get a higher score at this stupid tournament."

Eliana was troubled. Was that even allowed? And how bad would she look doing a beginner kata next to someone doing an intermediate one? "Well, good luck," she muttered. She tried to remember Sensei's words from the day before, but she wasn't feeling as good about the situation as she was before.

One by one, the other students in her division did their katas. One girl did her introduction way too quietly, and the judges couldn't hear. Another boy didn't have very stable stances, and he wobbled quite a bit. Eliana herself did ok, but she thought she could have done better. "It's not for my glory." she told herself as she bowed a final time to the judges and went back to take a seat.

Then the boy who had been next to her took his turn. His introduction to the judges commanded attention, and showcased his self -confidence. His moves were sharp, clean, and strong. She could even hear his gi snap as his arms went out and back to his belt. She just knew he was going to win this division with such a beautiful kata.

Until it happened. In one of his crossover moves, his left leg raised higher than it should have. Eliana knew this was for show, as the kata was not normally done this way. But in the process of this modification, the boy's supporting right leg buckled right under him! The boy fell to the ground, and for a moment he looked as surprised as all of the spectators. He quickly got up, and finished his kata with a red face and clearly absent mind. His pace had gotten off track, and there simply was no going back.

As he did his final bow to the judges, he took his seat beside
Eliana again.
"I'm sorry for what happened." Eliana whispered.
The boy just glared at her. Eliana knew he was just embarrassed,
so she didn't push it.

It was time for scores. The students rose to their feet and stayed in line. The judges called out the student's names, and each one took a step forward to receive their grades. As each student did so, the judges in the 3 corners held up their score cards, and the numbers were recorded by a man in the corner with a clipboard.

Eliana tried to keep track of all the scores, but there were just too many to average out in her head. Before she knew it, all students were back in one line, and the judges were calling out placements. The head judge in the front began, "Third place, Justin!" Everyone clapped as he stepped forward to bow and receive his medal. "Second place, Janet!" The girl stepped forward to bow and receive her trophy.

"This is it." whispered Eliana.

"First place, Eliana!"

Eliana's eyes grew wide in wonder, and she barely realized what was happening before she was in front of the judge, bowing and receiving her first place trophy.

After she was finished with kata, she found a place to sit where she could watch Jen and Kim in their sparring division. She had a while to go yet before she needed to gear up.

Everyone in this division had their gear on already, and it looked as if a couple matches had already passed. Luckily, she got to watch Kim's next. She smiled as she cheered for her.

Kim was going to be sparring a tall, lean man. She looked a bit intimidated. The two students bowed to the head judge, then to each other, then touched gloves.

"Hajime!" the judge yelled loudly.

Kim seemed to keep her distance at first. She knew with a taller opponent, she was at a disadvantage with kicks. She would have to move in and out quickly.

But the man she was sparring had no such plans of easing into the match. He quickly covered the distance with an elevated side kick as high as Kim's head! She barely had time to dodge the first kick before he executed a jumping turn back kick.

Kim quickly veered off to the side, praying to just make it through the match. Her opponent kept coming at her with fancy moves, and at one point he even chuckled as he toyed with her.

Eliana furrowed her eyebrows. If only everyone had been given the humility talk. This just wasn't fair!

Kim certainly didn't seem to be having fun. In fact, she was hoping her opponent would tire himself out, but that didn't seem to be the case. It was all she could do to avoid his assaults. Then she had an idea...

As the man moved in with another elevated side kick, she side-stepped to the left and delivered a swift punch to his gut.

"Break!" the judge shouted. "Judges call!" Two of the judges pointed to Kim with one finger. "One point," the judge said, pointing to Kim. "Hands up! Hajime!"

The man seemed bewildered. How could she have gotten a point in??

His ego seemed to be getting the better of him, as he tried more elaborate attack moves to cover the uneven score. Kim did her best to block what was too close, and stay away from his kicks. As he moved in with a turning back-fist, Kim quickly ducked under his leading arm and delivered a punch to his stomach again.

"Break!" the judge called again. "Judges call!" All three judges pointed to Kim with one finger again. "Two points!" the judge called, pointing to Kim. "Zero!" he called, pointing to the man. "Hands up! Hajime!"

Kim and the man both knew if Kim got the next point, she would be the winner. As the man concentrated on beating his opponent, Kim focused on relaxing. "Not for my glory, not for my glory." she whispered to herself.

In a final act of desperation to win, the man did a back layout, extending his legs to try to kick Kim as he landed.

Eliana gasped. "Move, move, move!" she called. "If he hits you, you'll get hurt!"

But Kim wasn't thinking at all. In fact, her mind was calm and clear. Without processing what was happening, she instinctively did a front roll, avoiding his kick, and immediately after landing, extended her left leg out into a back kick that hit the man squarely in the chest!

"Break!" the judge called. "Judges, call!"

All three judges, with smiles on their faces, pointed to Kim with two fingers.

"Two points!" the judge called, pointing to Kim. "Four-Zero! End of match!"

Kim was lost in thought as she lined back up. She couldn't believe what just happened!

"Bow to each other. Bow this way," the judge said. "Shake hands."

Eliana watched as several more matches took place. One by one, some students were eliminated and others moved higher up in the sparring rank. But before the final placing, she had to leave for her own sparring matches.

At the end of the day, all of the students left the tournament with a heightened sense of self-confidence. When all was said and done, it wasn't the fanciest katas or moves that placed – it was the ones done out of a humble spirit. Each learned that indeed, there were greater things than winning medals or trophies.

In fact, Kim reminded herself of this every time she dusted off her 2nd place sparring trophy from that day -

and her 1st place kata trophy from the tournament the following year -

and all of the other trophies she earned over the years -

and eventually, her black belt that she received years later.

Glossary of Japanese Martial Arts Terms

Do – The Way

Dojo – Karate School

Domo Arigato – Many Thanks

Gi – Uniform

Hai – Yes

Hajime – "Begin" Command

Karate-Do – Way of Empty Hand

Karate-ka – Student

Kata – Forms

Oss – Respectful Greeting (alternatively "osu", but commonly used as oss to depict pronunciation)

Rei – Bow

Senpai – Senior Belt

Sensei – Literally, "the one who has gone before." Commonly used to mean Teacher

Seiretsu – Line Up

Seiza – Sitting at Attention

Yame – "Stop" Command

Counting to 10 in Japanese:

Ichi

Ni

San

Shi

Go

Roku

Shichi

Hachi

Ku

Ju

For exclusive Parent/Instructor bonus content, please visit www.dmdtaekwondo.com

ABOUT THE AUTHOR

Ginny Aversa Tyler is a wife and homeschooling mother of three children. She is the owner and founder of DMD Tae Kwon Do, a Christian martial arts school near McKinney, Texas. (www.dmdtaekwondo.com)

Inspired by the endless lessons both God's Word and the martial arts have to offer, Ginny created the Kingdom Kicks book series for children so that they may tie their love of the martial arts to the lifelong guidance our Heavenly Father has offered.

Ginny's passion for teaching, not just her own children and students, is the basis for the Kingdom Kicks series, through which she wishes to inspire children all over the world to seek Biblical truths outside the walls of their home, school, and martial arts classes.

Made in the USA
Lexington, KY
08 May 2017